Happy Again

by Igor Plohl   illustrated by Urška Stropnik Šonc

I Like to Read®

HOLIDAY HOUSE • NEW YORK

Dear readers, physical impairment/disability
can't prevent you from being happy.
There are other things that can fill your heart with happiness:
help from loved ones, true friends, words of kindness,
love, and living life on the sunny side. —Igor Plohl

I LIKE TO READ is a registered trademark of Holiday House Publishing, Inc.

Text copyright © 2014 by Igor Plohl
Illustrations copyright © 2018 by Urška Stropnik Šonc
English translation copyright © 2021 by Založba Pivec
English translation by Kristina Alice Waller
Design by Grafični atelje Visočnik

First published in the Slovenian language in 2014 by Založba Pivec, Maribor, Slovenia.
First published in the English language as the picture book
LUCAS MAKES A COMEBACK in 2021 by Holiday House Publishing, Inc., New York.
This I Like to Read® edition first published in 2022.

Library of Congress Cataloging-in-Publication Data

Names: Plohl, Igor, author. | Šonc, Urška Stropnik, illustrator. | Plohl, Igor. Lucas makes a comeback.
Title: Happy again / by Igor Plohl ; illustrated by Urška Stropnik Šonc.
Description: First edition. | New York : Holiday House, 2022. | Series: I like to read
Adapted from the picture book Lucas makes a comeback (New York : Holiday House, 2021),
which was originally published in Slovenian in Maribor, Slovenia, by Založba Pivec in 2014 under the title:
Lev rogi najde srečo. | Audience: Ages 4-8. | Audience: Grades K-1.
Summary: "An easy-to-read story about Lucas the lion who learns how to
live life with a physical disability with help from his friends and family"— Provided by publisher.
Identifiers: LCCN 2022016116 | ISBN 9780823453764 (hardcover)
Subjects: CYAC: People with disabilities—Fiction. | Lion—Fiction.
Animals—Fiction. | LCGFT: Animal fiction. | Picture books.
Classification: LCC PZ7.1.P624 Hap 2022 | DDC [E]—dc23
LC record available at https://lccn.loc.gov/2022016116

ISBN: 978-0-8234-4766-4 (picture book)
ISBN: 978-0-8234-5376-4 (I Like to Read® edition)

Lucas is a happy lion.

One day Lucas falls.

He cannot walk
anymore.
Lucas is sad.

Can Lucas be
happy again?

He learns new ways
to do things.

He has a low sink.

He gets help too.

He gets a new bike.

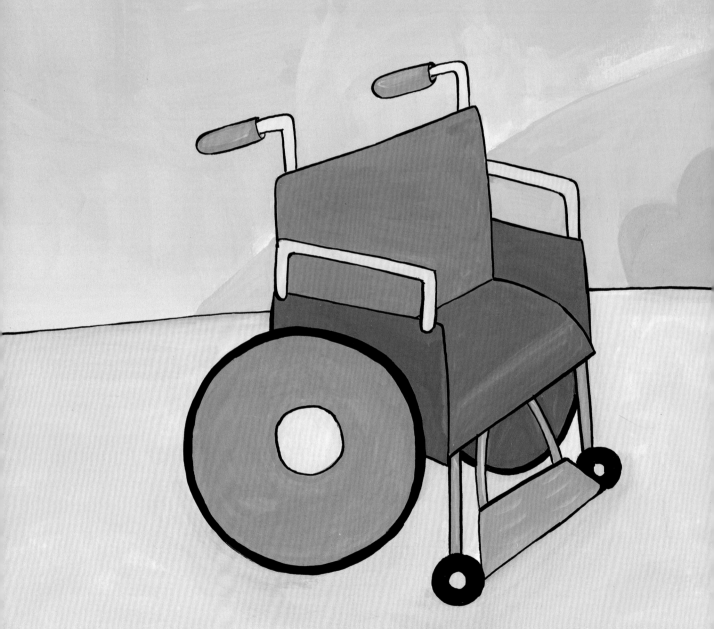

Friends visit.

They give him
a special car.
He can drive
to work.

Lucas is a teacher.

Lucas is almost happy again.
What more does he need?

He needs someone to love.
Now he is happy again.

Igor Plohl wrote this book.

Igor fell from a ladder—just like Lucas.

Igor learned new ways to do things too.